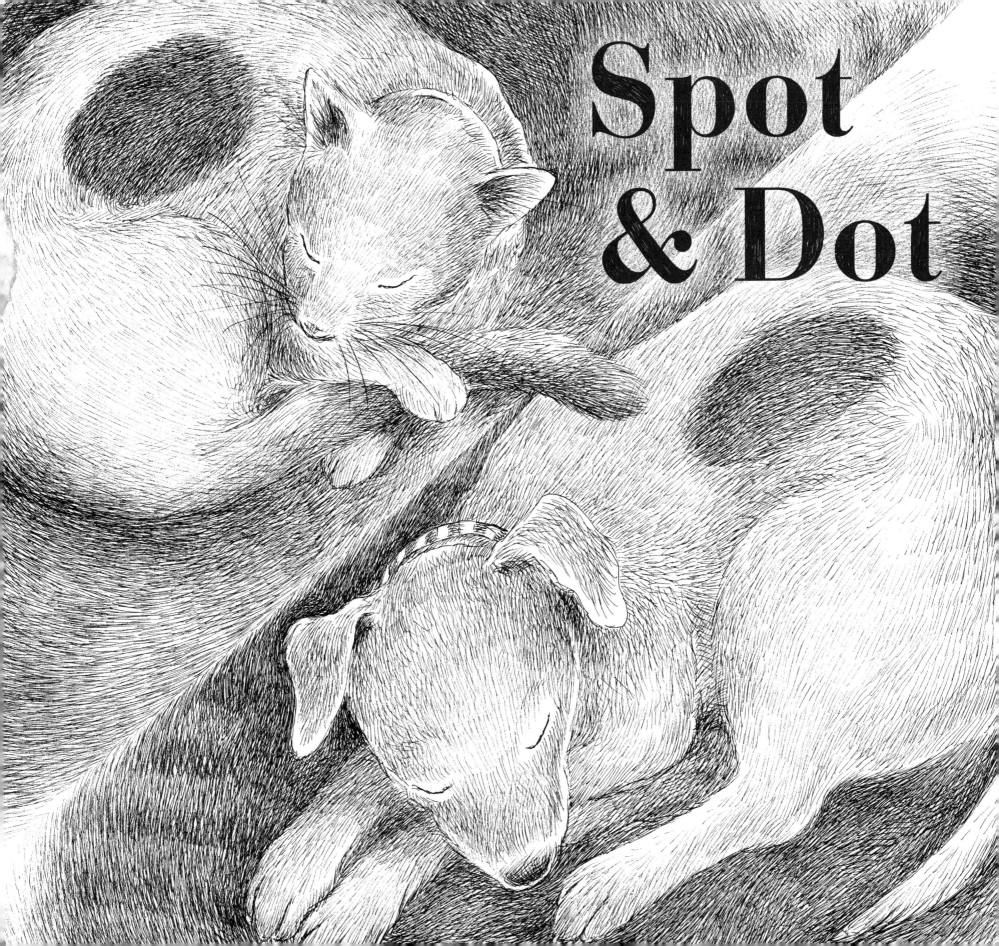

Spot
&
Dot

LITTLE SIMON
An imprint of Simon & Schuster Children's Publishing Division
1230 Avenue of the Americas, New York, New York 10020
First Little Simon hardcover edition August 2019
Copyright © 2019 by Henry Cole
LITTLE SIMON is a registered trademark of Simon & Schuster, Inc.,
and associated colophon is a trademark of Simon & Schuster, Inc.
For information about special discounts for bulk purchases, please contact Simon & Schuster
Special Sales at 1-866-506-1949 or business@simonandschuster.com.
The Simon & Schuster Speakers Bureau can bring authors to your live event. For more
information or to book an event contact the Simon & Schuster Speakers Bureau at
1-866-248-3049 or visit our website at www.simonspeakers.com.
Designed by Laura Roode
Manufactured in China 0519 SCP
2 4 6 8 10 9 7 5 3 1
Library of Congress Cataloging-in-Publication Data
Names: Cole, Henry, 1955– author, illustrator.
Title: Spot & Dot / Henry Cole.
Other titles: Spot and Dot
Description: First Little Simon hardcover edition. | New York : Little Simon, 2019. | Summary: In a
wordless picture book, Spot the cat goes out the open window and ventures through the city
with Dot the dog, seeking her home.
Identifiers: LCCN 2018053927 (print) | LCCN 2018057602 (eBook) | ISBN 9781534425569 (eBook) |
ISBN 9781534425552 (hc)
Subjects: | CYAC: Cats—Fiction. | Dogs—Fiction. | City and town life—Fiction. | Lost and found
possessions—Fiction. | Stories without words.
Classification: LCC PZ7.C67345 (eBook) | LCC PZ7.C67345 Sp 2019 (print) | DDC [E]—dc23
LC record available at https://lccn.loc.gov/2018053927

Spot & Dot

HENRY COLE

LITTLE SIMON
New York London Toronto Sydney New Delhi

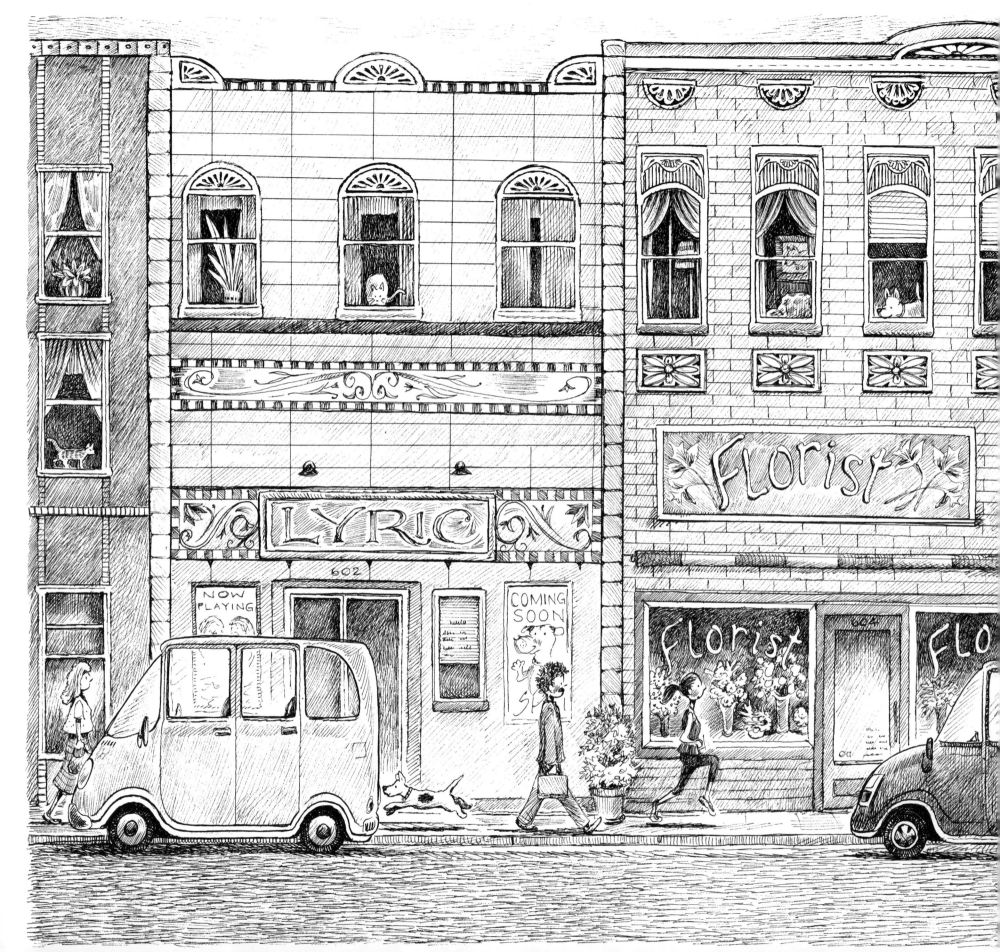